Renfrewshire
Council

The library is always open at
renfrewshirelibraries.co.uk

Visit now for
homework help
and free
eBooks.

We are the Skoobs and we love the library!

Phone: 0300 300 1188
Email: libraries@renfrewshire.gov.uk

For Lara and Theo ~ H.O.

For Hugh Cowling and Emma Lazenby,
two very cool cats, love Gwen x ~ G.M.

First published 2019 by Walker Books Ltd, 87 Vauxhall Walk, London SE11 5HJ • This edition published 2020 • Text © 2019 by Hiawyn Oram
Illustrations © 2019 by Gwen Millward • The right of Hiawyn Oram and Gwen Millward to be identified as the
author and illustrator respectively of this work has been asserted by them in accordance with the Copyright, Designs and
Patents Act 1988 • This book has been typeset in Triplex • Printed in China • All rights reserved. No part of this book
may be reproduced, transmitted or stored in an information retrieval system in any form or by any means, graphic,
electronic or mechanical, including photocopying, taping and recording, without prior written permission from the
publisher. • British Library Cataloguing in Publication Data: a catalogue record for this book is available from the British Library
ISBN 978-1-4063-9032-2 • www.walker.co.uk • 10 9 8 7 6 5 4 3 2 1

FLAT CAT

HIAWYN ORAM   illustrated by GWEN MILLWARD

WALKER BOOKS
AND SUBSIDIARIES
LONDON · BOSTON · SYDNEY · AUCKLAND

Sophie lived in a big white apartment
at the top of a tall building
in one of the busiest cities in the world.
With Sophie lived a beautiful cat
she called Jimi-My-Jim.

How Sophie spoilt Jimi-My-Jim.
Only the best was good enough for him ...
his dinners and toiletries, baskets and
blankets, glittering collars and cheeky clothes.

And you should have seen the playthings
Sophie heaped on that cat.
Most of the most spoilt children in the world
didn't have as many tantalising toys as Jimi-My-Jim.

Jimi did his best to be grateful.

He snuggled up when Sophie wanted to snuggle.
He played and performed when Sophie wanted him
to play and perform, and he always did what he was told.

Sophie thought everything was perfect between them and that Jimi had the perfect life for a cat.

And in one way he did but in another way he didn't because ...

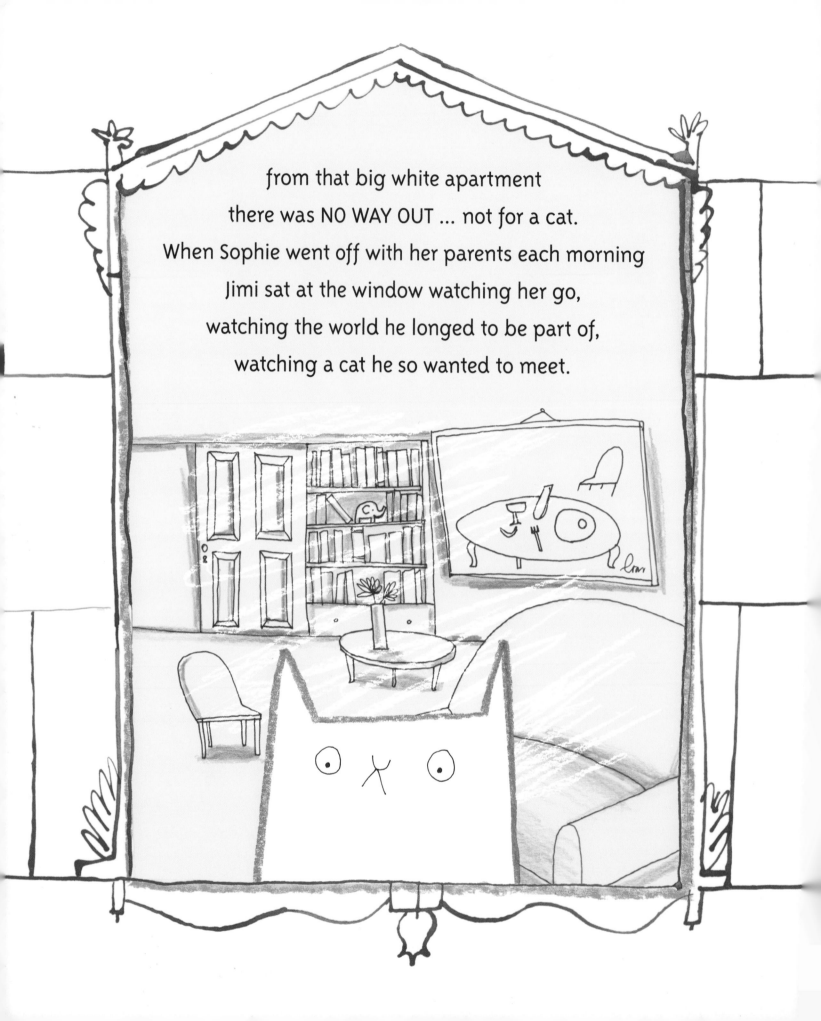

from that big white apartment
there was NO WAY OUT ... not for a cat.
When Sophie went off with her parents each morning
Jimi sat at the window watching her go,
watching the world he longed to be part of,
watching a cat he so wanted to meet.

Le Chat!

And as he watched for hours and days
something started to happen.
He began to feel FLAT. Flat as old flatbread.
Flatter and flatter and flatter ...
'til he LOOKED as flat as he felt!

"Forget Jimi-My-Jim," he tried to tell Sophie.
"Just call me FLAT CAT 'cause that's what I am.
LOOK! Flat as a cardboard cut-out cat."

And then one day Sophie was late for a singing concert in which she was the star and she and her mother were so flustered they dashed off, forgetting THE KEYS!

There they lay. Winking and glinting, inviting anyone stuck inside feeling flat as old flatbread to think ... *Who would ever know?*

And so ... putting on his jacket,
picking up the keys, Jimi stood on a chair,
unlatched the front door and ...

was out on the street ...
making straight for the cat
he so wanted to meet.

"Helloooo," she said.
"My name is Blanche.
You don't get out much, do you?
Well, I know this town like the
back of my paw. I'll be happy
to show you around."

So, side by side, through that city they went ...
up the uptown avenues,

down the downtown alleys,

through parks,

and palace kitchens,

all the way to the docks ...

for the evening's cat fight.

Blanche introduced Jimi
to her friends —
fat cats,
cool cats,
jazz cats,
boss cats,
scaredy cats,
alley cats,
cat burglars,
cat-nappers
and even a few dogs
who thought they were
the cat's whiskers.

By the time they got home Jimi didn't want
the evening to end and before he knew it
he'd invited his new friends
upstairs for a last lap
of cream.

Well, Sophie's apartment had seen a few parties, but nothing like this one!

While the jazz cats played,

the rest of them bopped and boogie-ed, rocked and rolled

and played Chase the Remote-Control-Mouse through every room ...

forgetting that sooner or later Sophie and her parents would come home.

And then they did!

Fast as lightning, the fat cats,
cool cats, jazz cats, boss cats,
scaredy cats, alley cats,
cat burglars, cat-nappers
and the dogs who thought they
were the cat's whiskers were

OUT OF THERE.

Jimi was left to face the telling-off alone.

Though not for too long.
When the apartment had been tidied
and all was calm, Sophie bundled
him up and took him to bed.

"I think I know why you did it," she whispered.
"You wanted the world, you wanted the wild
  and all I've done is smother you with THINGS."
"Hmmmm," purred Jimi.
"Well," said Sophie. "We're not allowed cat
  flaps in this building so I've thought
  of something else."

And a few days later Jimi found the last thing
he was expecting in his basket:
HIS OWN SET OF KEYS.

"But," said Sophie, "before you become a cat
of the world, do you promise to keep out of fights,
be in bed by ten and to NEVER bring your
dodgy friends back here again?"

"I do! I do!" purred Jimi.

And he kept his promise, that Jimi-My-Jim,
except for the night he got married to Blanche …

but that was all right.
Sophie was giving the wedding party!